WHO'S THE GANG ON OUR STREET?

Written by Susanne Gervay

Illustrated by Nancy Bevington

To fabulous kids, Kaiden, Zack and Madelyn.

There's a special gang
living on your street.
Come on, let's go find them!

Not a rock and roll gang with spikey hair.

But ... my hair is funky-punky.

Not a soccer gang with bright coloured uniforms.

But ... I love playing too.

Not a billycart gang who
race down the hill.

But ... I’m the fastest in the street.

Not a music gang with beating drums,
glittering cymbals and fancy flutes.

But ... I love to rock to the beat.

Not a gang of acrobats bounding and balancing.

But ... I love to hang upside down.

Not a street dancing gang
in a zig-zag squad.

But ... I can do the chicken dance too.

Not a birthday gang at a party
munching delicious treats.

But ... I love squishy bananas!

Squishy Bananas!
Blurgh, disgusting!

So who is the gang living on our street?

Let's find out!

Who are you?

Just
tell
us

You can see my gang everywhere.
We have loads of fun hanging out ...

rocking to a beat ...

tapping our toes.

My gang snack all the time ...

and teach each other new tricks.

We found you!

But ... who are YOU?

We're sulphur-crested cockatoos of course!

sQUaaARK

Facts about sulphur-crested cockatoos

Did you know?

Do you know parrots have been around for about 70 million years and live in warm climates across the world?

A funny, clever, playful parrot, the sulphur-crested cockatoo always entertains. These big white birds have pale yellow feathers under their wings and tails.

The mother lays 2-3 eggs in breeding time once or twice a year. BOTH parents look after the eggs and the chicks. The parents stay together all their lives. They love family.

Sulphur-crested cockatoos watch you with their big black eyes. The eyes of the girls have a reddish tinge.

When a sulphur-crested cockatoo is happy, scared, or emotional, the bright yellow crown of feathers wave and flutter.

Sulphur-crested cockatoos are very loud with high pitched screeching, they mimic all sorts of sounds and can speak to you.

Their favourite treats are seeds, grains, berries, nuts, leaf buds, some insects and even squishy bananas.

Most sulphur-crested cockatoos use their left leg like a hand. This makes them left-handed.

They fly as fast as 70 kilometres per hour. Nearly four times as fast as a grown-up can run.

Sulphur-crested cockatoos live from 20-40 years in the wild and even up to 100 years in captivity.

Match the facts

1. What food do they eat?

2. What temperatures do cockatoos like?

3. What colour eyes do they have?

4. How fast do they fly?

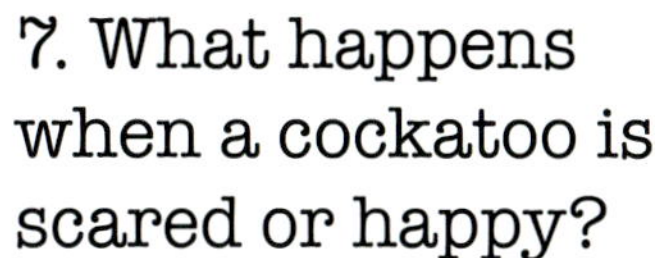

7. What happens when a cockatoo is scared or happy?

5. How many eggs do mother cockatoos lay?

6. What is the colour of sulphur-crested cockatoos?

8. Are they right or left handed?

9. Can cockatoos talk?

10. How many birthdays do cockatoos have?